Flotsam
and Jetsam

and the
GROOOF

For Doug, Alex, Jay, Hope and Holly
T. L.

For Mark and Julia
R. R.

First published 2008 by Walker Books Ltd
87 Vauxhall Walk, London SE11 5HJ

This edition published 2014

4 6 8 10 9 7 5 3

Text © 2008 Tanya Landman
Illustrations © 2008 Ruth Rivers
Cover illustration © 2014 Marta Dlugolecka

This book has been typeset in StempelSchneidler

Printed and bound by CPI Group (UK) Ltd, Croydon, CR0 4YY

British Library Cataloguing in Publication Data:
a catalogue record for this book is available from the British Library

ISBN 978-1-4063-5217-7

www.walker.co.uk

Flotsam and Jetsam

and the GROOOF

TANYA LANDMAN

illustrated by Ruth Rivers

WALKER
BOOKS

Scan the code to hear Tanya Landman
read the first chapter of this book

The new pet

Every day, an old man and a young boy walked the cliff path to the harbour where their wooden rowing boat waited for them, bobbing up and down in the water as though keen to be off.

They had always walked alone. But in the cold crisp sunshine of an autumn morning, the man and boy were followed by a new pet. Trotting eagerly at their heels, ears pricked and tail wagging, was a dog.

If the man and boy had paused for a moment and looked down from the cliffs, they would have

seen a little beach with an
upturned boat in the middle and an
old piece of drainpipe poking out of it. They
might have seen a whisper of smoke curling
through it, as if a cosy fire was burning inside.

But they didn't look. They didn't even glance
down. To them it was just a little beach, nestling
at the bottom of high cliffs: impossible to get to on
foot and not worth visiting by boat – too small to
bother with.

Only the dog caught the sharp scent of seaweed tea that drifted upwards on the morning breeze. He stopped and sniffed the air curiously.

The boy whistled, and at once the dog scampered after him.

When they reached the harbour, the dog settled himself on the wall, resting his head on his paws. He watched as the man and the boy rowed out to sea. When their little boat rounded the headland, the dog shut his eyes and began to doze, waiting patiently for their return.

The histle

Flotsam and
Jetsam lived on
a tiny beach that
snuggled against
the feet of towering cliffs.
Jetsam's hair was wild and knotted old
string. The top of Flotsam's bald head was
worn as smooth and round as a pebble.
Both had jet-black eyes peering out from
brown driftwood faces. Ropy legs ended
in chunky, toeless feet. Stringy arms
bore shapely hands, with nimble,
stick-like fingers.

The tiny beach had been their home
ever since a moonlit night long ago when
something had stirred in the inky depths of
the sea and they had drifted to the surface.
The tide had carried them in and laid them
down gently on the soft, welcoming sand.

The sea had many moods. Sometimes
a gentle breeze smoothed the surface of
the water and it would lie almost perfectly
still, dozing lazily in the bright sun like a
contented cat. Sometimes a wind whipped
the water into fearsome waves, and it
would grow wild, roaring as savagely
as an angry tiger.

But whatever the season, and whatever
its mood, Flotsam and Jetsam knew that
the sea was their friend.

Twice a day the tide went out. Sea anemones drew in their sticky fingers. Limpets sucked down tight on rocks. Crabs scuttled to hide in pools as the water ebbed away. Twice a day the sea returned, flooding rock pools and cooling sun-baked sand. There was a magical moment of high water when the sea paused and seemed to rest for a minute before the tide turned. And it was then that it would lay down a line of strange and wonderful things on Flotsam and Jetsam's little beach.

The sea had brought Flotsam and Jetsam the boat that they had made into a cosy house. It had carried the drainpipe that they used as a chimney, and the jam jars that they turned into windows. Their JA FA bed

had slid from a cargo
ship and their biscuit-tin table and drinks-
can chairs had been carelessly tossed
from ferries. Their only armchair was a
punctured football that had bobbed along
in the waves. The sea had even brought
them Sainsbury, a tiny hermit crab who
had lost his shell and now wore a silver
thimble which had rolled from the deck
of an ocean liner.

And one cold, crisp morning it brought them the most mysterious thing they had ever seen.

It was early autumn and the wind had begun to bite. All night it snapped and nibbled the waves into angry little peaks. Snug and warm in their JA FA bed, Flotsam and Jetsam slept soundly until midnight, when they were woken by a new and peculiar sound.

It wasn't the cry of a curlew or the cackle of a gull. It wasn't the quack of a duck or the piping of an oystercatcher. It wasn't even the bark of a fox from the clifftops. It was a wail that rose and fell with the wind. Each time there was a strong gust, the noise became piercingly shrill.

"Doesn't sound natural, does it?" whispered Flotsam fearfully. "It doesn't sound like something alive."

"'Tis not like something dead, neither. 'Tis not a ghostie." Jetsam tried to sound firm, but her voice wobbled when she spoke. "'Tis a creature. Must be. 'Tis an animal us has never heard of. A small one. I expect 'tis something quite harmless."

Just then the wind blew hard, and the wailing outside rose to a ghastly shriek.

"Doesn't sound small," said Flotsam. "Doesn't sound harmless, neither."

Jetsam – wide-eyed with fright – said nothing. They clutched each other's hands tight and wriggled deep down under the blanket and waited for morning.

By daybreak, the wind had dropped and the noise had stopped completely.

The sun was shining in a faint, half-hearted way through the jam-jar windows as if it had tired itself out during the long summer. There was a chill in the air that whispered a warning of cold days ahead.

Flotsam climbed out of the JA FA bed. Yawning, he fed the fire with lolly sticks and bits of driftwood, and put a tin can of water on to boil. As soon as it was hot, he dropped small pieces of dried seaweed into the water. When it smelt good and salty, he poured it into two empty limpet shells and carried them over to Jetsam.

"Is it raining?" she asked sleepily, rubbing her eyes.

"No."

"Is it drizzling?"

"No."

"Well, what *is* it doing?"

Flotsam sighed thoughtfully. His breath came out in a misty puff.

"'Tis puffing," he decided. "'Tis terrible cold."

"Us must wear our kin ocks, then."

The brightly coloured hiking socks had dropped from the rucksack of a hiker strolling along the cliff path, and fallen on to the beach

 below. Flotsam and Jetsam wore them wrapped tightly around their bodies, the toe end slung over their shoulders like a toga. They were very useful for keeping out the cold.

Muffled up against the chilly day, Flotsam and Jetsam set off to find what had been making the terrible noise during the night.

They walked the entire length of the beach. They looked in rock pools and searched the cave. They peeked under pebbles and peered behind boulders. But there was no sign of what had woken them up.

"Perhaps 'twas a bird," suggested Flotsam. "A bird what's gone and flown away now."

"Perhaps," said Jetsam, puzzled. "But it wasn't a bird us has heard before. It was most peculiar. Sure as petrels is petrels. Sure as kittiwakes is kittiwakes."

"It was," agreed Flotsam. "But 'tis gone now." Breathing a sigh of relief, he began to gather the treasures the sea had left for them. There were shells and fishing floats; pieces of net and cuttlefish bones; mermaids' purses and old tin cans. When his arms were full, he carried everything to the cave to be stored.

As he came back out, he saw that Jetsam had found something shiny.

 "What is it?" he asked as he got closer.

"'Tis a histle,"
announced Jetsam, and she put the gleaming silver object in his hands.

Flotsam read the writing on the side. "'Tis not any old histle," he said. "'Tis an ootba histle."

"'Tis very nice," said Jetsam.

"'Tis proper marvellous," agreed Flotsam.

There was a pause while they both looked at it. And then Jetsam said, "But what does it do? What's it for?"

Flotsam examined it. He peered through the hole at the top. He squinted through the hole at the bottom. He rubbed it. He sniffed it. He tapped it. Then he laid it carefully on the sand and sat down beside it. He cupped his bald head in his stick-like fingers and said quietly, "I is thinking."

For a very long time, Flotsam said nothing.

Jetsam gathered an armful of treasures and took them to the cave while Sainsbury scampered in and out of the waves. Flotsam didn't stir.

Jetsam gathered up lolly sticks and stacked them beside the boat-house fireplace while Sainsbury raced around in circles. Flotsam still didn't budge.

Jetsam made some warming seaweed tea and sat next to Flotsam while he drank it.

And at last Flotsam said, "I've thunk."

Jetsam, eyes wide, waited with excitement to hear what they were going to do with the ootba histle. But all Flotsam said was, "I doesn't know what 'tis for. 'Tis most mysterious."

"Oh." Jetsam was disappointed. But then she said, "Well … 'tis a nice, shiny thing. Us can hang it in the boat house. It will look nice, even if it doesn't do nothing."

She picked the histle off the sand.

A faint clunk came from inside.

"It has got something stuck in it," she said, giving it a shake. She peered inside. "'Tis a little ball. I don't think 'tis supposed to be in there."

She rattled the histle, but the ball wouldn't come out. The opening was too small for her to poke it, but it seemed possible that it might come out of the bigger hole if it was forced. If she had enough puff she could probably blow it out. Jetsam lifted the ootba histle to her lips, took a deep breath and blew.

It was as if
something had
exploded on the tiny beach. The
noise was so loud and so shocking that
Flotsam and Jetsam were thrown backwards
and landed, arms outstretched, in the sand.
Poor little Sainsbury was startled clean out

of his thimble. His wobbly, unprotected behind was exposed to the chilly air as he lay on his back with his legs flailing wildly.

It was some time before Flotsam and Jetsam managed to haul themselves upright. They helped the blushing crab back into his thimble, and then looked accusingly at the ootba histle.

"*That* was what was making the nasty noise in the night. The wind must have been blowing it. Horrid old thing," tutted Jetsam. She glared fiercely at it. "Us hasn't got no use for that. Sure as leaky cups is leaky cups. Sure as square wheels is square wheels."

"The sea wouldn't have brought it to us if it was just rubbish," said Flotsam. "It must be useful for something." He scratched his bald head thoughtfully, but try as he might he couldn't think of a single thing to do with it.

At that very moment, a herring gull swooped over their heads and landed in the waves. It wasn't as big as the black-backed gull that had once sat itself down in their chimney, but it was every bit as scary. It bobbed on the water, looking at them with its piercing yellow eyes. It wasn't a friendly look. Sainsbury ran up Flotsam's leg and tried to hide himself beneath the layers of kin ock.

"Oh! Stop it! Oh! Ow!" cried Flotsam as the crab's claws pricked his ropy legs. "Help! Get him off, Jetsam! Ow! *OW!!!* Help!"

Jetsam wasn't listening. Her eyes had narrowed. With a look of fierce determination on her face that would have sent any sensible creature scurrying to safety, she picked the ootba histle off the sand.

"Fingers and claws in ears," she commanded, clamping the shiny object between her lips. Flotsam and Sainsbury did as they were told. Clapping her hands hard to the side of her head, Jetsam marched towards the waves.

The gull gave a sneering cackle as she came closer. Jetsam took a deep breath and—

SCREEEEECH!

When Jetsam opened her eyes, the gull was lying flat on its back on the waves.

Shaking its head from side to side, the gull plucked its huge wings out of the water and struggled upright. Jetsam gave another blast on the ootba histle. The gull flapped hard and pulled itself clear of the waves. She blew again and the bird flew higher and higher and further and further away. Soon the dreadful creature was nothing more than a speck in the distance.

Jetsam gave one last, triumphant toot and then lowered the histle. She beamed as Flotsam and Sainsbury ran across the beach towards her.

"'Tis proper useful," Flotsam said happily. "I knew it must be. That's what 'tis for. 'Tis a seagull scarer!"

"'Tis fearsome powerful. 'Tis proper marvellous!" agreed Jetsam. "Us shan't have no more trouble with seagulls! Sainsbury shall be safe."

They threaded the histle onto a length of twine and Jetsam hoisted it onto her back like a rucksack in case they should need it again.

And then, feeling very happy, Flotsam and Jetsam sat leaning against the side of their boat house. Sainsbury scampered in and out of the sea as they watched the sun sink slowly beneath the waves.

The dog woke up suddenly, lifted his head and
looked around. No boat bobbed in the harbour.
The old man and the young boy had not returned,
and yet he was sure he had heard someone
whistling for him.

Getting to his feet, the dog jumped down
from the harbour wall. Ears pricked,
tail wagging, he trotted towards
the cliff path.

The grooof

That night Flotsam and Jetsam had just settled into their JA FA bed when they heard another strange sound.

It wasn't the rush of the sea, or the patter of rain. It wasn't even the noise of the wind blowing through the ootba histle.

This was a scratching and a scrabbling and it came from high up on the cliffs.

"What's that?" said Jetsam, clasping Flotsam's hand nervously.

"I doesn't know," he replied. "But 'tis coming closer."

It was true. The sound had started far above them, but as they listened it seemed to get nearer. There was a click and a clack of claws on rock. Then a pause, as if something was thinking, and planning its next move. A thud and another scramble followed as it made its way down the cliffs.

"'Tis a thing out there," said Flotsam nervously.

They listened as the scrabbling grew louder. Every so often, there was a clatter as whatever was making the noise dislodged loose stones and sent them rolling down the cliff face and onto the beach.

"'Tis a creature," said Jetsam. "A terrible big one. Sure as stingrays is stingrays. Sure as great white sharks is great white sharks."

They both paled at the thought of what was approaching. Poor little Sainsbury trembled so much that he overturned his wellington boot and sat blinking in a little

puddle of sea water.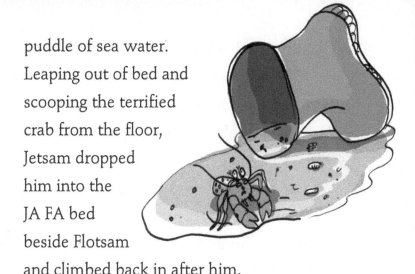
Leaping out of bed and
scooping the terrified
crab from the floor,
Jetsam dropped
him into the
JA FA bed
beside Flotsam
and climbed back in after him.

"'Tis all right," she said bravely. "Us has got the ootba histle. One blast shall drive that there beast away." She clenched it in her teeth and, putting her hands over her ears, blew with all her might.

But to their dismay, the ootba histle didn't drive the creature away. A joyful cry answered its shrill blast, and the scrabbling increased to a feverish intensity. There was a sudden desperate yelp as if the thing outside had lost its footing, and an avalanche of stones pelted the boat-house roof.

The distressed howl of something falling pierced the night air. There was a dreadful heavy thud as it hit the sand. Then silence.

"Does you think 'tis hurt?" asked Jetsam.

"Must be," answered Flotsam.

"Maybe us should go and see." Jetsam's voice quavered as she spoke.

"Maybe us should."

Flotsam and Jetsam exchanged terrified glances. Neither of them climbed out of the cosy JA FA bed to see if the large – and possibly dangerous – creature needed their help.

Just as Jetsam was gathering all her shreds of courage together a loud noise echoed across the beach.

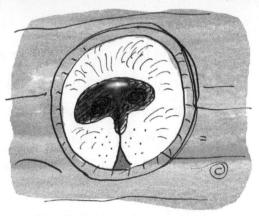

"'Tis alive!" she exclaimed. For a moment, she was delighted. But only for a moment. Because suddenly a very big, very black nose was pressed damply against the jam-jar window. Flotsam and Jetsam were terrified. The nose drew in a deep sniff – so deep that it seemed to suck all the air from the boat house. The creature let out another deafening cry.

"EEEEEEEEEEEEEEEEEEEEEEEK!!" Flotsam and Jetsam screamed in pure terror. Which seemed to make the beast even more excited. It started scratching the boat-house walls with its monstrous claws, dislodging the jam-jar window nearest the JA FA bed and sending it rolling into the sea. It thrust its nose through the gap and drew another breath, sucking Jetsam's stringy hair into its left nostril like a giant vacuum cleaner, before giving a great wet sneeze. And then powerful paws started to dig in the soft sand beside the boat house. Through the hole in the wall Flotsam and Jetsam could see a shower of tiny pebbles being thrown high into the air.

"'Tis trying to get in!" gasped Flotsam.

"'Tis going to eat us!" yelled Jetsam.

To their horror, a hole appeared beneath the boat-house wall and a huge paw reached in.

Seizing Sainsbury, Flotsam and Jetsam
leapt from the JA FA bed and fled to the far
end of their house. But – with one sniff of
its powerful nose – the beast knew that they
had moved. It began to circle the boat house.

They stood, frozen with fear. Clasping
each other by the hand they asked helplessly,
"What shall us do? *What shall us do?*"

Any moment now, the beast would find
the boat-house door. And then…

"Then us is done for, good and proper!"
wailed Flotsam. He grabbed a lolly
stick, brandishing it like a
sword. "Us shall have
to defend
ourselves."

Jetsam seized a piece of driftwood to use as a club. "Us is not going to be supper for a big beast if us can help it!" she said.

Sure enough, in a matter of seconds, the big wet nose poked through the boat-house door. It was followed by a big hairy head.

Flotsam and Jetsam waved their weapons. But they didn't have time to attack. Sainsbury – small though he was – leapt into action before them. He scuttled across the floor, a glint of steely determination in his beady black eyes.

"No, Sainsbury!" gasped Flotsam.

But it was too late. Opening his claws wide, Sainsbury jumped at the animal's great nose.

With a howl of pain, the creature snatched back its head. It did it so swiftly that brave little Sainsbury didn't have time to let go. He was yanked through the door and away into the night.

With a shriek
of *"Sainsbury!"*
Flotsam and
Jetsam sped after him.

A vast hairy monster was on their little
beach. If it had been standing still it would
have been terrifying enough, but the beast
was thrashing its great head from side to
side so violently that the sand beneath
its feet seemed to rock.
Its howling whine was
so loud that the cliffs
appeared to tremble
in response.

Sainsbury was clamped to the
end of its nose. It swung its head one
way and then the other in an
attempt to dislodge him,
but still Sainsbury held
on tight. Only when the
beast braced its legs and

shook itself hard from head to
tail did Sainsbury lose his grip.
He soared through the air in a great arching
curve and splashed into the waves. The
monstrous beast bounded after him.

"No!" shrieked Flotsam and Jetsam
together.

To their astonishment, the animal
stopped. It turned and looked at them, ears
pricked, head on one side as if awaiting
further instructions.

"Talk to it," whispered Flotsam, nudging
Jetsam hard.

"I doesn't know what to say," she hissed.

"Think of something," replied Flotsam.
"Quick. Before it tries to eat Sainsbury."

Jetsam looked at the beast. The beast
looked at Jetsam. For a very long time she
didn't say anything. She tried. She tried very
hard. She opened her mouth. But all that
came out was a faint gasping noise.

At last she managed
a croaky, "Good evening.
'Tis a nice night. Moon's
proper full, isn't it?"

The creature wagged its
tail. Jetsam hoped that was
a good sign.

"I has never seen a
beastie like you," she said in
a quavering voice. "What kind
of beastie is you?"

"Grrrrrrr," said
the animal.

"Grrrrrrr," repeated Jetsam. "You is a
grrrrrrr, is you?"

The animal barked, "Ooof!"

"Ooof!" copied Jetsam. "Grrrrrrr ... ooof.
So that's what you is, is you? A grooof.
I hopes you is a friendly grooof."

Not far away, Flotsam could see
Sainsbury, emerging from the waves.

His scuttle was rather lopsided, and he swayed from side to side as if he'd been dizzied by his heroic attack.

Slowly, carefully, while Jetsam and the grooof eyed each other, Flotsam edged towards Sainsbury and picked him up, holding him tightly against his chest to keep him safe.

Then Flotsam walked carefully back
to Jetsam. "Shall us go inside?" he whispered.

"I thinks us should try," replied Jetsam.
"Us might be safer there."

Keeping their eyes firmly fixed on the
grooof, Flotsam and Jetsam took a step back
towards the boat-house door. The grooof
took a step forward. They stepped back.
The grooof stepped forward. Back. Forward.
Back. Forward.

The trouble was that each of the grooof's
steps was twice as long as Flotsam's and
Jetsam's. They were at the entrance to the
boat house when it caught up and stood
towering over them, snorting hot breath
down on Flotsam's bald head and Jetsam's
knotted string hair.

The grooof peeled its lips back in a scary
grin. Its very large, very sharp teeth glinted in
the moonlight before it lowered its mouth to
Jetsam's face. She gave a little squeal of terror.

And then the grooof's long pink tongue snaked forward and smeared her with a friendly lick.

"Eeuw!" she exclaimed, wiping drool off her face.

There was a wet sound as the grooof's tongue greeted Flotsam, sliding damply over his nose and cheeks.

"Yuck!" he said.

"It seems like a harmless grooof," said Jetsam uncertainly. "I hopes it won't hurt us."

"I hopes you is right," agreed Flotsam.

They edged carefully backwards through the door. The grooof followed. There was no way of stopping him.

Once inside, the hairy visitor seemed to fill their entire house. Standing with its head pressed against the ceiling, its tail thumped noisily against the walls.

Exhausted by all the excitement, Jetsam made for the football armchair, muttering weakly, "I is quite worn out. I needs to sit."

There was a thud behind her. Jetsam turned. The grooof had sat down and was wagging its tail, sending yoghurt pots full of dried seaweed rolling across the floor.

Jetsam sighed. "Boiling bladderwrack!" she complained to Flotsam. "Now us is going to have to tidy up!"

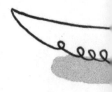

But Flotsam's eyes were shining with excitement. "I is thinking," he said. "You just said sit, and it sat. Try something else."

"What?"

"Tell it to do something. Go on."

Jetsam stared at the grooof.

"Stand," she tried.

The grooof stood.

"Sit."

The grooof sat.

"Lie down."

The grooof lay down.

"Go to sleep."

The grooof lowered its head onto its paws
and closed its eyes.

Flotsam and Jetsam exchanged surprised but rather pleased glances.

Flotsam yawned. "'Tis terrible late," he said. "Us should all go to sleep."

But first they tiptoed around the boat house setting things straight. Flotsam stood Sainsbury's wellington boot upright, filled it with sea water and tucked the little crab into its toe. Jetsam stacked the scattered yoghurt pots neatly against the wall. Edging back past the huge sleeping body of the grooof, they climbed into the JA FA bed.

"I'm glad 'tis not ferocious," whispered Jetsam, looking at the vast hairy creature.

"So is I," agreed Flotsam. "But 'tis too big. I doesn't know what us is going to do with it."

"Us can worry about that in the morning. 'Tis time to sleep now," said Jetsam firmly.

They pulled the blanket up to their chins and snuggled down.

On the little beach, nothing else moved. Nothing stirred but the sea. Nothing disturbed the silence but the gentle lapping of the waves, and the rise and fall of soft, contented breathing that drifted out of the doorway of the boat house.

When the old man and the young boy returned
from their fishing trip, the dog was nowhere to be
seen. They called until their voices were hoarse
and their throats sore, but he did not come trotting
eagerly towards them.

Eyes blurred with tears, the young boy trudged
behind the old man homewards along the cliff
path. It was too late to look for the dog now.
They would search again in the morning.

A game
of fetch

 Flotsam was woken
by the slap of a warm,
wet tongue on his
cold, bald head. He
sat up and was rewarded by the grooof's
sharp bark of greeting. It was followed by
the long, low rumbling of the creature's
enormous and empty stomach.

Sainsbury – who had begun to clamber
out of his red wellington boot – heard the
sound, and immediately burrowed back
down and pulled a piece of seaweed over
his head.

Climbing from the JA FA bed, Flotsam squeezed nervously past the grooof towards the fire. He stoked it and put the water on to boil. Then he offered their visitor a seaweed sausage. With great care, the grooof picked it gently from Flotsam's hands, and then threw its head up in the air and swallowed its breakfast in one gulp.

Flotsam and Jetsam drank limpet shells full of tea and gobbled down some bladderwrack crispies. Then Jetsam strapped the ootba histle to her back and they were ready to discover what the sea had brought them in the night.

When it realized they were going out, the grooof leapt up and bounded through the door so fast that it sent Flotsam spinning across the boat house and crashing into Jetsam.

"I don't know what us is going to do," grumbled Jetsam. "'Tis a nice enough beast. But 'tis too enormous. Sure as seals is seals. Sure as great grey whales is great grey whales."

Flotsam called for Sainsbury, but the little crab's courage seemed to have deserted him. He had dug himself deep into the toe of his boot. It was only when Flotsam offered to carry him that Sainsbury finally emerged.

Together they left the boat house, Sainsbury riding high on Flotsam's shoulder, clasping his ear firmly in his claw. It made Flotsam's eyes water but he didn't complain. As soon as they stepped through the door, the grooof sprang towards them,

jumping up and down with excitement and showering them with sand.

The grooof wasn't huge, but Flotsam and Jetsam were very small. To them it seemed that an animal the size of an elephant was galumphing around on their tiny beach. Nervously they began their search for treasures, holding each other tightly by the hand.

They hadn't gone far when the grooof picked up a large piece of driftwood and dropped it in front of them.

"Very nice," Jetsam said.

The grooof stood looking at her, wagging its tail, eyes shining bright.

"'Tis for me, is it?" she asked uncertainly.

The grooof barked.

"I suppose 'tis trying to be helpful," Flotsam said. "Perhaps 'tis gathering wood for the fire."

"Oh," said Jetsam. "Well... 'Tis proper

kind. Thank you." Releasing Flotsam's hand, she bent to pick up the stick, but as soon as she did so, the grooof seized the other end in its teeth.

It pulled, yanking so hard that Jetsam fell flat on her face.

She let go. So did the grooof.

Jetsam got to her feet. The stick lay on the beach between them.

The grooof stood watching her. Slowly Jetsam reached for the driftwood. As soon as her fingers touched it, the grooof clamped the other end in its teeth.

She let go again. So did the grooof.

"Now look here," she said sternly. "You can't go giving folks things and then snatching them away. 'Tisn't polite. 'Tisn't nice. You leave that stick alone."

The grooof sat down heavily in the sand. Fixing it with a hard stare, Jetsam bent to pick up the driftwood. The grooof didn't move. Her fingers closed around the stick.

"Eurgh!" she said in disgust. "That there grooof has made it all slobbery. 'Tis slimy and horrid. Sure as lugworms is lugworms. Sure as lumpsuckers is lumpsuckers. It needs a good wash."

She threw it into the waves, where the sea could rinse it clean. With a yelp of delight the grooof leapt after it, snatched it from the sea, and dropped it back at Jetsam's feet with a thud.

"What did you do that for?" she said, puzzled.

"I thinks the grooof wants you to throw it," suggested Flotsam.

"What for?"

"Perhaps 'tis a game."

"Oh." Jetsam looked at the grooof. "Is *that* what you wants? You wants to play, does you?"

The grooof barked happily.

So while Flotsam gathered treasures, Jetsam threw the stick for the grooof. The only trouble was, her stringy arms were short, and she couldn't throw the stick very far. Soon Jetsam was worn out. The grooof wasn't. Its enthusiasm for the game seemed inexhaustible.

Jetsam sat on the sand and tried to get her breath back. "My arms is aching!" she called to Flotsam. "'Tis your turn!"

On the other side of the beach, Flotsam had found an old ball. It had been blown there from a bigger beach and the wind had wedged it safely against the cliffs.

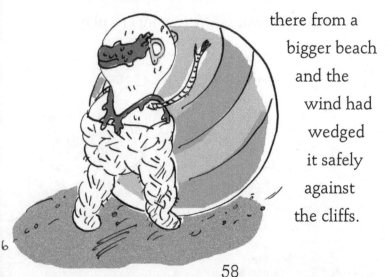

Flotsam was rolling it across the sand to put it safely in the cave.

When the grooof saw the ball, it leapt to its feet, showering Jetsam with sand. It bounded towards Flotsam, who squealed in alarm. Sainsbury, trying to hide behind his claws, let go of Flotsam's ears and plopped down onto the ground. Scooping him up in one arm, Flotsam fled for the safety of the rocks.

But the grooof wasn't interested in Flotsam or Sainsbury.

The ball rolled towards the sea, and the grooof chased after it. When it caught up, it pushed the ball with its nose and flipped it across the beach towards Jetsam. When it got near her, the grooof sat down. It looked at Jetsam with its head on one side, and then looked once more at the ball.

"You wants to play with that now, does you?" asked Jetsam.

The ball was too large for her to pick up and throw, so she gave it a good, hard kick instead. Large as it was, it was still light enough to roll a long way. The grooof chased after it, and steered it back with its nose. But instead of stopping so that Jetsam could take another kick, it steered around her in a tight circle and then sped away across the beach, its mouth open in a wide grin.

"Hey!" she shouted. "You come back here. 'Tis my turn."

The grooof didn't come back. It ran around the beach in great, teasing circles, barking joyfully.

"Right," said Jetsam. "That's the game now, is it?"

She sped after the grooof as fast as her ropy little legs could carry her.

When the grooof turned, Jetsam ran
at the ball, stealing it from under the creature's
nose and kicking it towards Flotsam.

"Come on, Flotsam! Come on, Sainsbury!
'Tis your go!"

With Sainsbury now riding on his head,
Flotsam couldn't run very fast, but he managed
to reach the ball and give it a shove. Sainsbury
bounced up and down in excitement. Flotsam
sped after it, but the grooof was quicker. In
seconds it had the ball back and was bounding
across the sand, inviting them to follow with
wild, excited barks. They ran after it in a glorious
game of chase that went from one end of the
beach to the other. Then they paused for breath.

The grooof lay, the ball between its front paws, waiting for the game to begin again.

"'Tis terrible funny," laughed Jetsam. "'Tis marvellous amusing. Come on, shall us get that ball back?"

"Us shall," said Flotsam. "You goes that side, us shall go the other. Us shall corner the grooof by that there rock pool."

They sped towards the grooof, ropy little legs pumping furiously. Sainsbury blinked and held tight to Flotsam's ears as the wind whistled past his beady black eyes.

The grooof saw them approaching from either side. It backed up against the rocks. They had it cornered. But it wasn't going to give the ball away without a struggle. It grabbed it in its teeth and crouched low, ready to leap over their heads.

But at that moment there was a *pop!* and a hiss and the grooof, surprised, dropped the ball and sat down, staring at it.

Flotsam and Jetsam skidded to a halt.

"Oh dear," said Jetsam sadly. "'Tis that terrible whooshing. That horrible hooshing. That means the ball has got a hole in it."

Before their eyes the ball got smaller and smaller until it was left squashed and with no bounce at all. The grooof whined sadly. A little tear oozed from Sainsbury's eye and plopped onto Flotsam's nose.

"Oh, poor grooof," said Flotsam.
"Poor Sainsbury."

"'Tis a terrible pity. Oh, 'tis a terrible
shame. Sure as skates is skates. Sure as
narwhals is narwhals."

Flotsam cupped his bald head in his stick-
like fingers and said quietly, "I is thinking."

There was a long pause while they all
stared at the punctured ball. But at last
Flotsam said, "I've thunk." He stood up,
turned and sat back down, settling his
bottom into the squashed hollow of the
deflated ball.

"I thinks us can both be comfy now. That
there grooof has gone and made us another
armchair."

Flotsam was right. On cold winter
evenings they wouldn't have to take turns
in the only comfortable chair. They could
have one each and sit together, cosy and
warm, by the fire.

They pulled it into the boat house and left Sainsbury happily bouncing from one chair to the other, while outside, Flotsam and Jetsam took turns throwing sticks for the grooof.

And later, feeling very happy, they all sat leaning against the side of their boat house, and listened to the sea as they watched the sun sink slowly beneath the waves.

The old man and the young boy searched for the
dog all around the village. They knocked on the
door of every single cottage, and asked if anyone
had seen him. No one had. After a long day's
searching, the old man and the young boy headed
sadly for home.

As they walked along the cliff path at sunset,
the boy heard a bark from somewhere below him.
He looked down. The dog was there on the sand!
He was going into an upturned boat through a
crack in its side!

"Look, Grandpa!"

The old man looked. Way below them was a tiny beach – impossible to reach on foot.

"We can get there in the boat," said the old man. "But not tonight. I don't trust those rocks in the dark." He put his hand gently on the boy's shoulder. "We'll row out and fetch him tomorrow."

Giants

 Flotsam was woken once more by the slap of a warm, wet tongue on his cold, bald head. He sat up.

Bright, golden light flooded in through the gap left by the dislodged jam jar. It streamed under the wall where the grooof had dug a hole. It burst through the door as if eager to tell them that this was the last warm day of the year and they should hurry outside to make the most of it.

"'Tis sunning," he announced. "Sunning good and proper."

Flotsam started to make the breakfast, which was a tricky task with the grooof taking up so much room. He stoked the fire and made the tea. He was just reaching for the bladderwrack crispies when he tripped over the grooof's tail and sent several pots flying.

Campion marmalade, sea pink jelly and sugar kelp cream hurtled through the air and splatted across the floor in a horrible sticky mess.

"Oh no!" wailed Jetsam. "It will take all morning to clear that up!"

But before she could start, the grooof had gone over to examine it. He sniffed, stuck out a long pink tongue and started licking it up.

"Good grooof!" called Jetsam encouragingly. "Go on, have some more."

The grooof did. Before long it had lapped up the whole horrid mess. Jetsam was delighted and gave the creature a friendly pat.

"I suppose you has your uses, even if you is too big," she said. "You makes a good mop."

But Sainsbury wasn't very pleased. Sea pink jelly was his favourite food, and it made him terribly sad to see so much of it disappearing into the grooof's cavernous mouth.

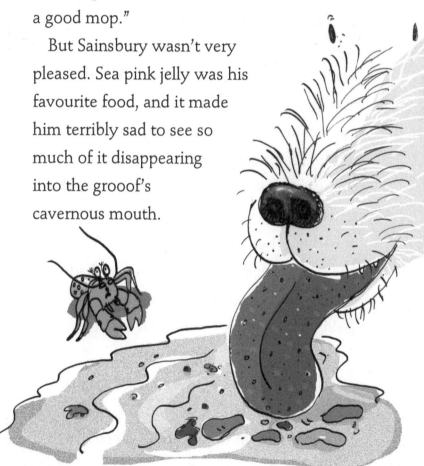

When they'd had breakfast, Jetsam fastened the ootba histle onto her back, and they all set off to discover what the sea had left them on the little beach. Sainsbury rode on Flotsam's shoulder again, clinging on to his ear. The grooof bounded around them in large circles, barking with excitement. It snatched up a stick and dropped it at Jetsam's feet. She threw it as they wandered along looking for treasures.

The sea had brought them bits of rope and twine, plastic bottles and shiny drinks cans. And in the biggest, deepest rock pool it had left them a jam jar. It was exactly the same size as the one the grooof had dislodged and was hanging in the water, held up by a bubble of air that was trapped inside.

"The sea has brought us a new window," said Flotsam. "That was kind."

He bent down to pick it up. As he did so,

the air escaped and made a rude noise. Jetsam gave him a stern look.

"'Twasn't me," said Flotsam. "'Twas this here jar."

He emptied the water out while Jetsam gave the grooof's stick a particularly energetic throw.

At that moment, disaster struck. The twine which fastened the ootba histle to her back snapped. Jetsam gave a little cry of dismay as the shiny ootba histle dropped onto the sloping rocks, slid down and then plopped into the rock pool. The biggest, deepest rock pool.

They watched in horror as their shiny treasure – the fearsomely powerful seagull scarer – spiralled gently downwards and came to rest on the sand at the bottom.

"What can us do?" wailed Jetsam.

"Us can get it out again," said Flotsam with rather more confidence than he felt.

"But how?" Jetsam asked, wringing her hands. "Us can't reach it. 'Tis too far down."

Just then, Sainsbury gave a squeal and pinched Flotsam's ear.

"Ow! Sainsbury, stop it! You is hurting!" protested Flotsam.

"He has had a thunk!" said Jetsam, lifting the crab off Flotsam's shoulder. "Does you want to try getting it?"

Sainsbury wiggled his thimble in agreement.

"What does you want to do?"

The crab didn't answer. He ran around in several little circles as if he couldn't contain his excitement. Then he extended his legs and bounced up and down on the spot like a runner getting ready for a big race. Suddenly he took off, scuttling towards the rock pool.

Taking an almighty leap into the air, he turned a somersault before plopping into the water.

Jetsam gasped, but Flotsam said, "'Tis all right. He can breathe down there. He can get it out for us."

They watched Sainsbury scurrying happily across the sandy bottom. He reached the ootba histle and waved cheerfully up at them. Then he took it in his claws.

It was no good. The histle was small, but Sainsbury was smaller. With a huge effort, using both claws he could just about lift it off the sand. But the only way out of the pool was by climbing up the seaweed that grew on the sheer rocks at the sides.

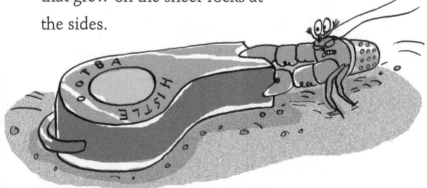

Doing that with the ootba histle pinched in one claw was impossible.

Sadly, Sainsbury pulled himself out of the pool empty-clawed. Defeated, he sat on the rocks and blinked away a tear.

"Never mind, Sainsbury, you did your best," soothed Jetsam. "And you was very brave to try."

"You was," agreed Flotsam. "You is a very courageous crab."

The grooof gave a loud bark. Sainsbury scuttled up Flotsam's arm and grabbed his ears.

Jetsam looked at the grooof. "What is you trying to say?" she asked.

The grooof barked again.

"Does you want a turn?"

Another ear-piercing bark was the reply.

"Go on, then," she said. "Have a go."

The grooof's attempt was even less successful than Sainsbury's. It started by

lowering its head into the water and trying
to get the histle in its teeth. It couldn't
reach, and a stream of air bubbled from its
nostrils. When it pulled its soaking wet head
out, it sneezed and then shook itself so hard
that everyone was drenched. The grooof
tried again, lowering a paw into the water
and scraping hopefully at the histle. But all
he managed to do was stir up clouds of sand
that almost hid it from view.

"Stop! Stop!" ordered Jetsam. "Us shall never find it that way."

The grooof stared at the histle and barked at it crossly.

"Now you be quiet," said Jetsam. "It won't come out just because you tells it to."

Flotsam sat down on the rocks and cupped his bald head in his stick-like fingers.

"I is thinking," he said. Desperate as she was to get the ootba histle back, Jetsam said nothing. She knew Flotsam thunk good thoughts and so she left him in peace to think them. She walked along the beach, throwing the stick for the grooof.

Flotsam picked up the jam jar and dunked it upside down in the water. He looked at the bubble of air he'd trapped.

"I've thunk," he said. Putting the jar back on the rocks, Flotsam picked up some lengths of twine that the sea had laid down on the beach. Choosing two large stones, he tied them to the soles of his toeless feet.

He plucked Sainsbury off his shoulders and handed him to Jetsam, then pulled the jar over his head. Winding a length of twine around the rim and tying it tight, he passed the ends under his armpits and tied a knot across his chest.

"How does I look?" he asked Jetsam, who was staring at him open-mouthed.

"You looks … strange," she said.

Without any explanation, Flotsam handed one end of the long piece of twine to Jetsam. He took the other end in his hand, and told her, "Don't let go."

Then, to Jetsam's amazement, he stepped off the edge of the rocks and into the pool.

Flotsam's driftwood body would have floated, but with stones tied to his feet he sank straight to the bottom. Jetsam watched with alarm, but to her surprise he landed upright, looked up at her and smiled broadly. It was then that she noticed the trapped air.

"He can breathe!" she told the grooof excitedly. "What a clever thunk!" She grinned at Flotsam and watched as he walked across the sand like a deep-sea diver.

When he reached the ootba histle, he tied the end of the twine through the loop and then gave it a hard tug. Taking this as her signal, Jetsam hauled away until the histle was pulled up and out of the pool.

But Flotsam was still at the bottom.

She peered over the side and called to him, "How is you going to get out? I hope you is not stuck. That would be terrible. Sure as beached whales is beached whales. Sure as oils spills is oil spills."

She watched anxiously. But Flotsam was untying his stone sandals. As soon as the last knot was loosed, the air in the jar carried him upwards and he popped to the surface like a cork. Heaving himself out onto the rocks, he was met by an excited Sainsbury.

"Does the histle still work?" asked Flotsam.

"I shall test it," said Jetsam, lifting it to her lips.

But she didn't have time to blow it. To her surprise she heard a whistling sound from far out at sea.

The grooof lifted its head and barked loudly.

Flotsam and Jetsam peered into the distance. And then – to their utter horror – a wooden rowing boat rounded the headland.

Their eyes widened.

"'Tis a boat!" quailed Jetsam.

"'Tis coming here!" wailed Flotsam.

"Does you see what is in it?"

"GIANTS!!!!"

Without another word, they grabbed
Sainsbury and fled to the boat house.

Dropping the crab into his wellington boot, Flotsam and Jetsam dived into the JA FA bed and hid beneath the blanket.

The grooof stayed on the beach, and in between its joyful yelps Flotsam and Jetsam could hear the slow, regular sound of oars being pulled through the water. A thud as the boat struck sand. Two loud splashes as the giants climbed out. A dragging scrape as they pulled the boat onto the beach.

The grooof was barking and one of the giants was laughing and saying, "Good dog! Good boy! I'm so glad we found you!"

A deeper, louder voice said, "He seems well enough. Come on. Let's take him home."

Flotsam and Jetsam could hear the smaller giant's boots thud on the timber as he climbed back into the boat. The clack of the grooof's claws followed. There was a scraping as the bigger giant began to push the boat back down the sand.

But suddenly there was a splash, a few thudding bounds, and the grooof was inside the boat house, ripping the baby's blanket off the JA FA bed with its teeth and grabbing Flotsam and Jetsam by the legs.

"Eeeeeeeeek!" they screamed as they were carried across the beach in the beast's huge jaws.

But they were stunned into terrified silence when the grooof dropped them both into the small giant's lap.

"Brought you a present, has he?" asked the bigger giant as the grooof stood and stared at them expectantly.

The smaller one peered at the wave-worn wood and string. "It's nothing, Grandpa," he said, puzzled. "Just a bit of old flotsam and jetsam."

He picked up the knotted tangle, and was about to drop it on the floor of the boat. But then he took a closer look. He had seen something like it once before, being carried shorewards by the tide. He remembered the moonlit night long ago when he had made out a face – no, two faces – peering up at the stars. He had thought it was just a trick of the light…

He looked at the upturned boat. Noticed the old bit of drainpipe poking out of it.

The bigger giant lifted the grooof back into the boat and began once more to push away from the beach.

"Wait, Grandpa!" The small giant climbed out and walked thoughtfully across the sand. Gently, carefully, he laid the knotted tangle of driftwood and string down; and then, without another word, he turned and went back to the water's edge. Climbing into the boat, he patted the grooof and took an oar in his hands. Pulling together, the two giants rowed away.

Flotsam and Jetsam had to sit in their football armchairs and drink several shells of strong, sweet seaweed tea to recover from the shock. But when at last their nerves had steadied, they set about mending the boat house. They replaced the jam-jar window that the grooof's nose had dislodged. They filled in the hole that it had dug under the boat-house wall, and stacked the pots and jars its tail had scattered. They set everything straight while Sainsbury scampered around the beach, wagging his thimble in sheer delight that the monstrous grooof had finally gone.

And then, feeling very happy, they all sat leaning against the side of their boat house, and listened to the sea as they watched the sun sink slowly beneath the waves.

The old man, the young boy and the dog walked home along the cliff path.

The old man walked without stopping, the dog trotting obediently at his heels. But when they got to the top, the boy paused for a moment. He wondered what he might see if he looked down.

A little beach with an upturned boat in the middle? An old piece of drainpipe poking out of it? A whisper of smoke curling through it, as if a cosy fire was burning inside?

Perhaps it was best not to look.

Instead, he thrust his hands deep in his pockets and walked briskly to catch up with his grandfather.

And so the beach remains unnoticed and undisturbed, which is just as well.

It is the whole world to Flotsam and Jetsam and Sainsbury.

You can make your own Flotsam and Jetsam figures at home. Visit **www.tanyalandman.com** to send Tanya photos of what you make and to hear more from Flotsam and Jetsam.

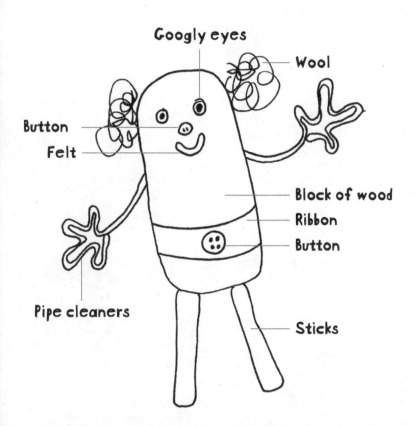

Googly eyes

Wool

Button

Felt

Block of wood

Ribbon

Button

Pipe cleaners

Sticks

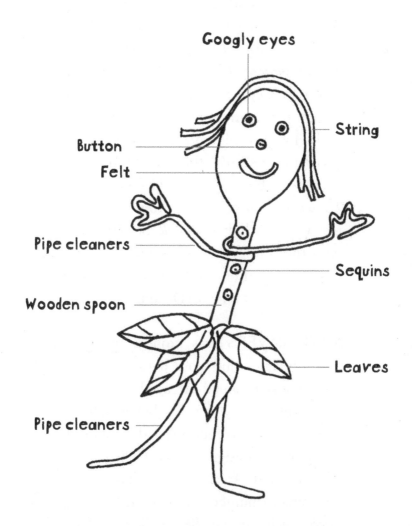

Googly eyes

String

Button

Felt

Pipe cleaners

Sequins

Wooden spoon

Leaves

Pipe cleaners

TANYA LANDMAN is the author of many books for children, including *Flotsam and Jetsam*, *Flotsam and Jetsam and the Grooof*, *Flotsam and Jetsam and the Stormy Surprise*, *The World's Bellybutton*, *The Kraken's Snore*, *Mary's Penny* and three Sam Swann movie mysteries, and she won the Red House Children's Book Award for *Mondays are Murder*, the first of ten murder mysteries about the intrepid Poppy Fields. Tanya has also written four books for teenagers, including *Buffalo Soldier*, which won the Carnegie Medal. Since 1992, she has been a part of Storybox Theatre. Tanya lives with her family in Devon.

RUTH RIVERS was brought up in the East Midlands and now lives in London. She almost dropped art aged fourteen as she wanted to be a vet – but luckily she was persuaded to continue and went on to study graphic design at Exeter College of Art and Design. She has illustrated a number of children's books, including *The Biggest Bible Storybook* by Anne Adeney and *Matty Mouse* by Jenny Nimmo.